Flip! Flup:

and

Go For It!

Maverick

Early Readers

'Flip! Flap!' and 'Go For It!'
An original concept by Katie Dale
© Katie Dale 2022

Illustrated by Antonella Fant

Published by MAVERICK ARTS PUBLISHING LTD
Studio 11, City Business Centre, 6 Brighton Road,
Horsham, West Sussex, RH13 5BB
© Maverick Arts Publishing Limited May 2022
+44 (0)1403 256941

A CIP catalogue record for this book is available at the British Library.

ISBN 978-1-84886-874-8

www.maverickbooks.co.uk

This book is rated as: Pink Band (Guided Reading)
It follows the requirements for Phase 2 phonics.
Most words are decodable, and any non-decodable words are familiar,
supported by the context and/or represented in the artwork.

Flip! Flap!
and
Go For It!

By Katie Dale

Illustrated by
Antonella Fant

The Letter A

Trace the lower and upper case letter with a finger. Sound out the letter.

Around,
up,
down

Down,
up,
down,
lift,
cross

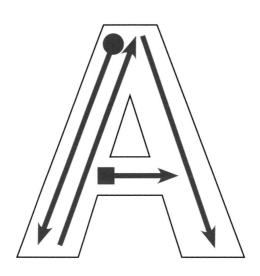

Some words to familiarise:

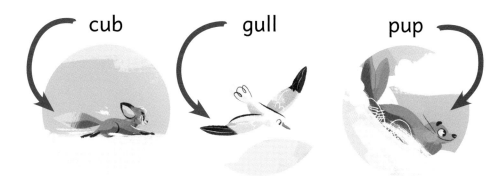

cub   gull   pup

High-frequency words:

the   is   I

Tips for Reading 'Flip! Flap!'

- Practise the words listed above before reading the story.

- If the reader struggles with any of the other words, ask them to look for sounds they know in the word. Encourage them to sound out the words and help them read the words if necessary.

- After reading the story, ask the reader what Fin was good at.

Fun Activity

Run on the spot as fast as you can!

Flip! Flap!

The cub is quick.

That is fun!

Flip flap...

The gull is quick.

That is fun!

The pup is quick.

Flip flap...

...Flip! Flap!

The Letter O

Trace the lower and upper case letter with a finger. Sound out the letter.

Around

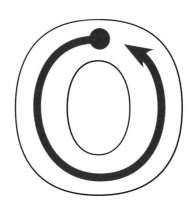

Around

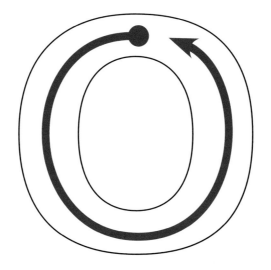

Some words to familiarise:

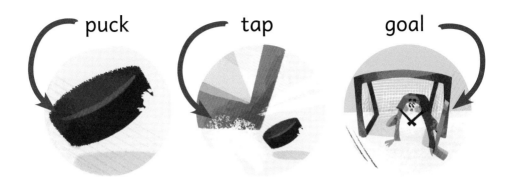

puck   tap   goal

High-frequency words:

the   go   no   it

Tips for Reading 'Go For It!'

- Practise the words listed above before reading the story.

- If the reader struggles with any of the other words, ask them to look for sounds they know in the word. Encourage them to sound out the words and help them read the words if necessary.

- After reading the story, ask the reader who scored the goal.

Fun Activity

Discuss what other games you can score a goal in.

Go For It!

Get the puck!

Go, Mel, go!

Tap the puck!

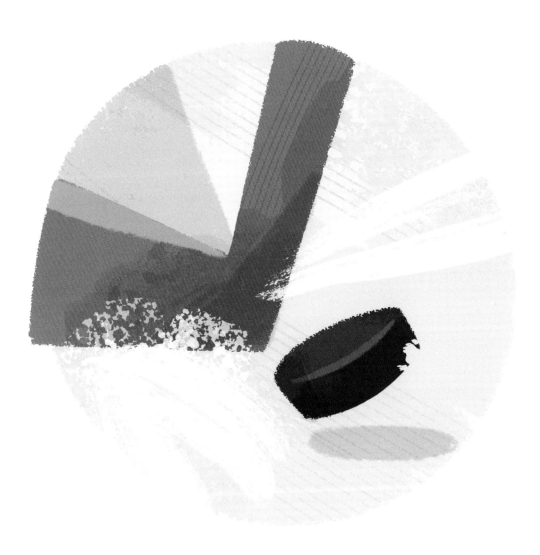

Go, Tom, go!

Pass the puck!

Go, Dan, go!

Goal!

31

Book Bands for Guided Reading

The Institute of Education book banding system is a scale of colours that reflects the various levels of reading difficulty. The bands are assigned by taking into account the content, the language style, the layout and phonics. Word, phrase and sentence level work is also taken into consideration.

Maverick Early Readers are a bright, attractive range of books covering the pink to white bands. All of these books have been book banded for guided reading to the industry standard and edited by a leading educational consultant.

Pink
Red
Yellow
Blue
Green
Orange
Turquoise
Purple
Gold
White

To view the whole Maverick Readers scheme, visit our website at www.maverickearlyreaders.com

Or scan the QR code above to view our scheme instantly!